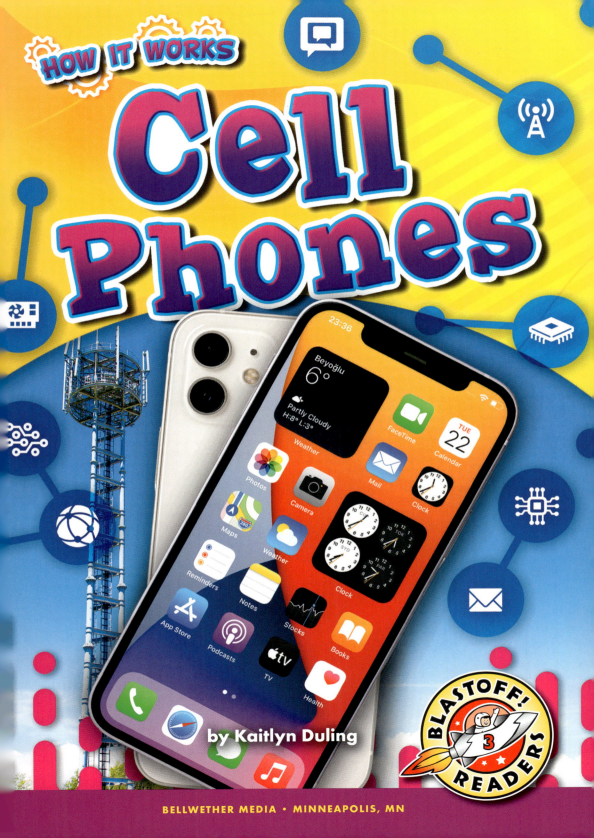

HOW IT WORKS

Cell Phones

by Kaitlyn Duling

BELLWETHER MEDIA • MINNEAPOLIS, MN

Blastoff! Readers are carefully developed by literacy experts to build reading stamina and move students toward fluency by combining standards-based content with developmentally appropriate text.

LEVELS

Level 1 provides the most support through repetition of high-frequency words, light text, predictable sentence patterns, and strong visual support.

Level 2 offers early readers a bit more challenge through varied sentences, increased text load, and text-supportive special features.

Level 3 advances early-fluent readers toward fluency through increased text load, less reliance on photos, advancing concepts, longer sentences, and more complex special features.

★ **Blastoff! Universe**

Reading Level

Grade K — Grades 1–3 — Grade 4

This edition first published in 2022 by Bellwether Media, Inc.

No part of this publication may be reproduced in whole or in part without written permission of the publisher. For information regarding permission, write to Bellwether Media, Inc., Attention: Permissions Department, 6012 Blue Circle Drive, Minnetonka, MN 55343.

Library of Congress Cataloging-in-Publication Data

Names: Duling, Kaitlyn, author.
Title: Cell phones / by Kaitlyn Duling.
Description: Minneapolis, MN : Bellwether Media, Inc., 2022. | Series: Blastoff! Readers: How it works | Includes bibliographical references and index. | Audience: Ages 5-8 | Audience: Grades 2-3 | Summary: "Simple text and full-color photography introduce beginning readers to how cell phones work. Developed by literacy experts for students in kindergarten through third grade"-- Provided by publisher.
Identifiers: LCCN 2021049242 (print) | LCCN 2021049243 (ebook) | ISBN 9781644875995 (library binding) | ISBN 9781648346743 (paperback) | ISBN 9781648346101 (ebook)
Subjects: LCSH: Cell phones--Juvenile literature.
Classification: LCC TK6564.4.C45 D85 2022 (print) | LCC TK6564.4.C45 (ebook) | DDC 621.3845/6--dc23/eng/20211012
LC record available at https://lccn.loc.gov/2021049242
LC ebook record available at https://lccn.loc.gov/2021049243

Text copyright © 2022 by Bellwether Media, Inc. BLASTOFF! READERS and associated logos are trademarks and/or registered trademarks of Bellwether Media, Inc.

Editor: Betsy Rathburn   Series Design: Jeffrey Kollock   Book Designer: Gabriel Hilger

Printed in the United States of America, North Mankato, MN.

Table of Contents

What Are Cell Phones? 4
How Do Cell Phones Work? 6
The Future of Cell Phones 18
Glossary 22
To Learn More 23
Index 24

What Are Cell Phones?

Cell phones are devices that help people **communicate**. People all over the world use cell phones.

People use cell phones to make calls and send messages. Some cell phones have games and other **apps**!

How Do Cell Phones Work?

Cell phones were made to make and receive calls while traveling. Every cell phone has a **microphone**.

Callers dial a number. They speak into the microphone. The phone turns the caller's voice into electrical **signals**.

microphone

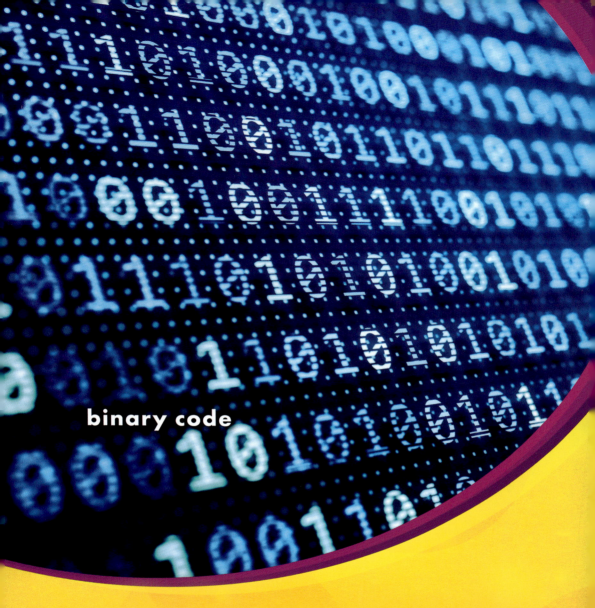

binary code

The electrical signals travel to a **microchip** inside the phone. It turns the signals into strings of numbers called **binary code**.

The cell phone's **antenna** then sends the code out as **radio waves**.

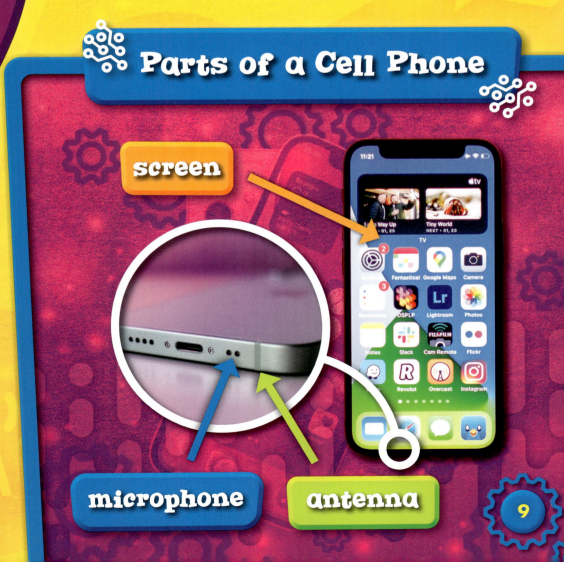

Parts of a Cell Phone

screen

microphone

antenna

The radio waves travel through the air. They go to antennas on **cell sites**.

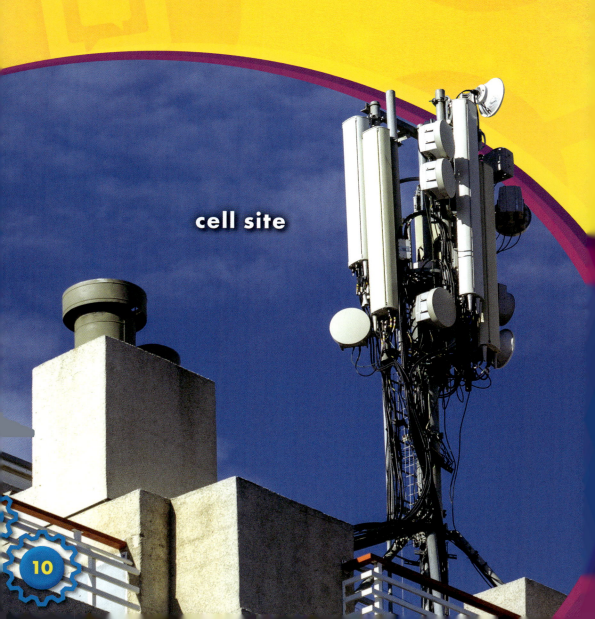

cell site

Cell sites are built on tall towers and rooftops. They are also built on flagpoles and other high places.

If a caller is far away from a cell site, the connection may be weak. The call may be **dropped**.

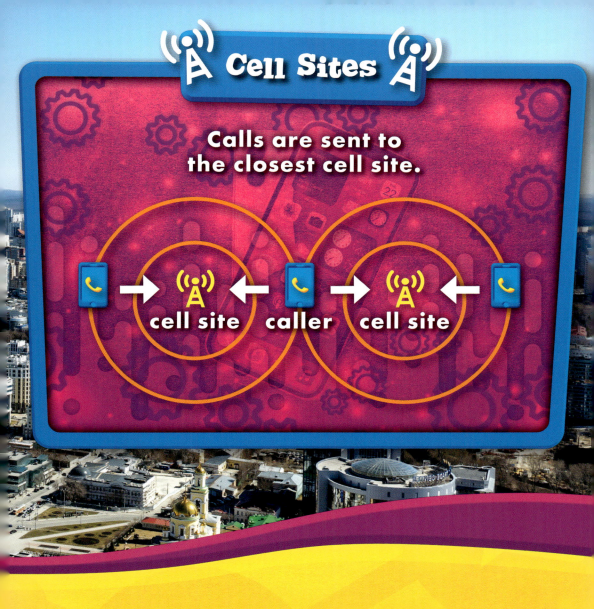

More cell sites can help create stronger connections. Most cities have many!

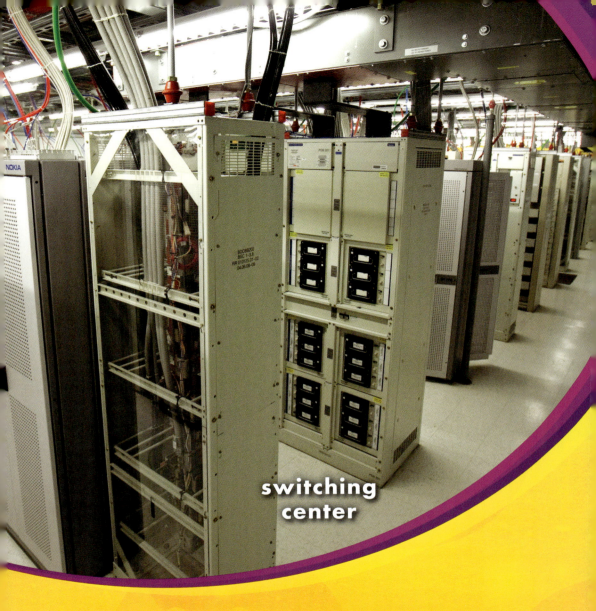

switching center

The cell site sends the call to its **switching center**. The switching center sends the call to a cell site near the **receiver**.

Then, the receiver's phone rings. They are connected to the caller!

Making A Call

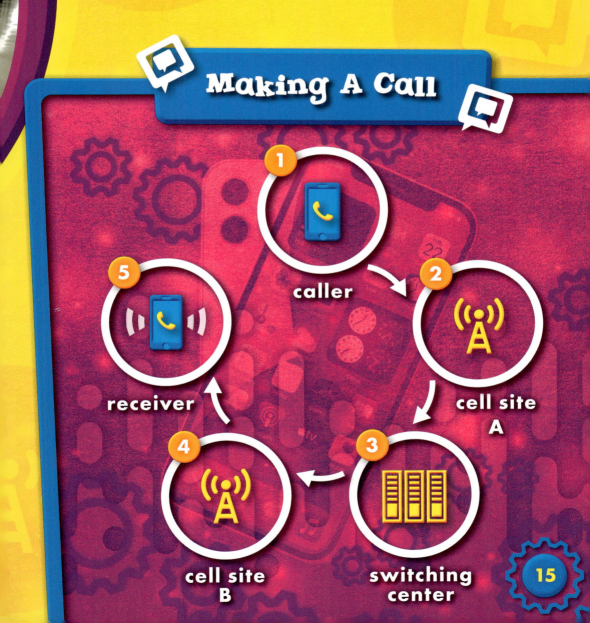

Sometimes, phones switch between cell sites. This happens if the caller is traveling.

The call moves to a different cell site. This frees up space on the other site for new callers.

The Future of Cell Phones

Today's cell phones are powerful tools. They do not only make calls. They are also **smartphones**!

Future phones will continue to do many jobs. They will do their jobs faster than today's phones.

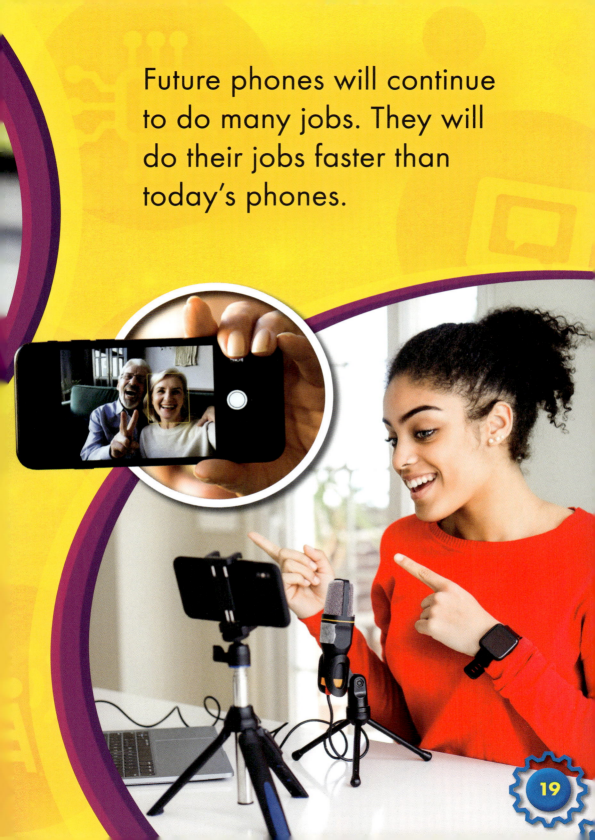

Future phones may look different. Their screens could fold or stretch. They could even be see-through!

Question

What do you think future cell phones will be able to do?

Researchers are even working on phones controlled by our brains. Future cell phones are full of possibilities!

Glossary

antenna—a device that sends and receives radio waves

apps—programs such as games and internet browsers; apps are also called applications.

binary code—a system that represents data using 0s and 1s

cell sites—places that send and receive signals from cell phones

communicate—to send and receive information

dropped—ended unexpectedly, usually because of a weak signal

microchip—a very small part of a cell phone that holds information

microphone—the part of a cell phone that picks up sounds

radio waves—energy waves that are used for long-distance communication

receiver—a person who gets a call

signals—the patterns of sounds sent from a phone's microphone to its microchip

smartphones—cell phones with advanced features such as internet access and apps

switching center—the part of a cell site that sends calls to other cell sites

To Learn More

AT THE LIBRARY
Bethea, Nikole Brooks. *Cell Phones*. Minneapolis, Minn.: Jump!, 2019.

Dinmont, Kerry. *Communication Past and Present*. Minneapolis, Minn.: Lerner Publications, 2019.

Pettiford, Rebecca. *Computers*. Minneapolis, Minn.: Bellwether Media, 2022.

ON THE WEB

FACTSURFER

Factsurfer.com gives you a safe, fun way to find more information.

1. Go to www.factsurfer.com.

2. Enter "cell phones" into the search box and click 🔍.

3. Select your book cover to see a list of related content.

Index

antenna, 9, 10
apps, 5
binary code, 8, 9
callers, 6, 12, 15, 16
calls, 5, 6, 12, 14, 16, 18
cell sites, 10, 11, 12, 13, 14, 16
communicate, 4
connection, 12, 13
future, 19, 20, 21
games, 5
making a call, 15
messages, 5
microchip, 8
microphone, 6
parts, 9
question, 21
radio waves, 9, 10
receiver, 14, 15
researchers, 21
screens, 20

signals, 6, 8
smartphones, 18
switching center, 14

The images in this book are reproduced through the courtesy of: Yalcin Sonat, front cover; robtek, p. 3 (left phone); ShiwaID, p. 3 (middle phone); Kaspars Grinvalds, p. 3 (right phone); insta_photos, pp. 4-5; Marc Bruxelle, p. 5; Hadrian, p. 6 (inset); Happy Together, pp. 6-7; cybrain, pp. 8-9; Daria Gromova, p. 9 (close-up); Karlis Dambrans, p. 9 (phone); Jordi C, pp. 10-11; Maksim Safaniuk, p. 11; Timofeev Vladimir, pp. 12-13; John W. Adkisson/ Stringer/ Getty Images, pp. 14-15; Roman Samborskyi, p. 16 (inset); Lewis Tse Pui Lung, pp. 16-17; Daniel Krason, pp. 18-19; fizkes, p. 19; Krakenimages, p. 19; Thomas Andreas/ Alamy, pp. 20-21; ALDECA studio, p. 23.